This book belongs to:

SYDNEY

The forgetful bunny

A little bunny story

PaRragon

Bath·New York·Singapore·Hong Kong·Cologne·Delhi·Melbourne

Four little bunnies live under the roots of a big, old oak tree in Dingle Wood.

This is Rocky.

This is Fern.

This is Blackberry.

And this is Daisy.

Daisy is a forgetful little bunny. Once, she even forgot the food for the bunnies' picnic!

This is Daisy's story.

One sunny day, Daisy woke up feeling really excited. "I'm sure today's a special day," she said. "But I can't remember why!"

The other bunnies looked at each other and smiled.

They knew what day it was, but they didn't want to tell Daisy – not yet, anyway.

"Daisy," said Fern, "please could you collect some packages from Fergie Frog, Sammy Squirrel, Monty Mouse, and Mrs. Bumble?"

"I'd love to," said Daisy, hopping up and down with excitement.

So, Daisy set off toward Lily Pond to meet Fergie Frog. She hadn't gone far when Fern called out, "When you've finished, meet us at Harebell Corner and don't forget!"

"Don't worry," said Daisy. "I've tied a knot in this bunch of grass to help me to remember."

She held the grass up for the others to see.

Then, she hoppity-hopped away and was soon out of sight.

Blackberry, Fern, and Rocky
giggled to themselves.
They had a special surprise
planned for their friend.

Daisy hopped deeper and deeper into Dingle Wood. After a while, she stopped under a tree for a rest. She looked at the bunch of grass in her paw.

"That looks yummy," thought Daisy.

She was just about to have a nibble,
when she suddenly remembered.
"I tied this knot to remind me to meet
the other bunnies – but where?"
she wondered.

So, Daisy set off once again into
the wood, trying to remember where
she had to meet the other bunnies.

Soon, she came to the little bridge that crossed over
Lily Pond. And there, she met Fergie Frog!

"I thought you'd forgotten you were coming to see me," croaked Fergie.

"Oh, no, I did remember," said Daisy. "But I'm not sure why!"

"What a forgetful bunny you are," chuckled Fergie.

He gave Daisy a package, wrapped up in a big lily pad.
Then he dived into the pond and swam away under the bridge.

"Daisy!" shouted a voice. "Over here!"

It was *Sammy Squirrel*, sitting on a branch of his tree.
"Did you forget you were coming to see me?" he said.

"Of course, I didn't," said Daisy. "I think we were going
to collect nuts together, weren't we?"

"No, Daisy," laughed Sammy. "We did that last week!
You really are a forgetful bunny!"

He scampered down and handed her a small package.
Something was wrapped in a crinkly leaf with a pretty flower on top.

"Here you are," he said. "You were meant to come and collect this."

Then, waving good-bye
with his big, bushy tail,
Sammy ran back to his
little tree house.

Daisy continued to
hoppity-hop into Dingle Wood.

"I wonder who I'm supposed
to meet next?" she thought.

"You're meant to meet me!"
said a small voice.

It was Monty Mouse!
"Where have you been?" he asked.
"Did you forget where I live?"

"Oh, don't be silly," giggled
the bunny. "I was going
to give you one of these
packages, wasn't I?"

"Oh, no, Daisy," said Monty.
"I was meant to give you a package!"

And, with that, the mouse gave Daisy
something tiny, wrapped in red poppy petals.

"Oh, thank you,"
said Daisy. But, before she could
say another word, Monty had
scampered away.

Just then, Mrs. Bumble buzzed by.

"Hello, Daisy," she said, cheerily. "I've got something special for you."

"Thanks," said Daisy. "I love balloons!"

"Now, weren't you meant to meet your
friends somewhere?" asked the bee.

Suddenly, the balloon slipped out of Mrs. Bumble's tiny hands and floated away.

"Oh, no!" cried Daisy and hopped off after it, as fast
as her bouncy, bunny feet would let her.

Daisy jumped up and tried to catch the balloon, but it just kept floating away. She chased after it and was very careful not to drop anything on the way!

And, each time she caught up with the balloon, off it flew again –
as if someone was pulling the string.

The excited bunny hopped, skipped, and jumped all the way to...

... Harebell Corner!

What a surprise Daisy got. There were Blackberry, Fern, and Rocky,
all holding onto the end of the balloon string!

"We thought you would forget to meet us here," they laughed.
"But we knew you would follow the balloon."

"So, that's why I tied the knot in the grass," said Daisy.

"To remind me to meet you at Harebell Corner!"

"But I did remember to collect your packages," said Daisy, proudly.

"Those are your packages," Blackberry giggled. "Today's your birthday."

Daisy laughed.
"Oh, how could I forget my
own birthday!" she said.
"What a forgetful bunny I am."

Then, Rocky, Blackberry and Fern led Daisy to a clearing,
where they had made her a surprise birthday picnic.

Suddenly, Fergie Frog, Sammy Squirrel, Monty Mouse, and Mrs. Bumble appeared.

"Happy Birthday," they all sang together.

Next, it was time for Daisy to open her presents. There was a lily bracelet from Fergie Frog, a cherry necklace from Sammy Squirrel, and a tiny berry ring from Monty Mouse.

It was a great party! There was a lot of *yummy* food and they all played
Daisy's favorite games – pass the acorn and *musical mushrooms!*

So Daisy, the forgetful bunny, had a wonderful birthday party
that she would never forget – well, not for a few days, anyway!